Dear Parents:

Congratulations! Your child is taking the first steps on an exciting journey. The destination? Independent reading!

STEP INTO READING® will help your child get there. The program offers five steps to reading success. Each step includes fun stories and colorful art or photographs. In addition to original fiction and books with favorite characters, there are Step into Reading Non-Fiction Readers, Phonics Readers and Boxed Sets, Sticker Readers, and Comic Readers—a complete literacy program with something to interest every child.

Learning to Read, Step by Step!

Ready to Read **Preschool–Kindergarten**
• big type and easy words • rhyme and rhythm • picture clues
For children who know the alphabet and are eager to begin reading.

Reading with Help **Preschool–Grade 1**
• basic vocabulary • short sentences • simple stories
For children who recognize familiar words and sound out new words with help.

Reading on Your Own **Grades 1–3**
• engaging characters • easy-to-follow plots • popular topics
For children who are ready to read on their own.

Reading Paragraphs **Grades 2–3**
• challenging vocabulary • short paragraphs • exciting stories
For newly independent readers who read simple sentences with confidence.

Ready for Chapters **Grades 2–4**
• chapters • longer paragraphs • full-color art
For children who want to take the plunge into chapter books but still like colorful pictures.

STEP INTO READING® is designed to give every child a successful reading experience. The grade levels are only guides; children will progress through the steps at their own speed, developing confidence in their reading.

Remember, a lifetime love of reading starts with a single step!

 Published in the United States by Random House Children's Books, a division of Penguin Random House LLC, 1745 Broadway, New York, NY 10019, and in Canada by Penguin Random House Canada Limited, Toronto, in conjunction with Disney Enterprises, Inc.

Step into Reading, Random House, and the Random House colophon are registered trademarks of Penguin Random House LLC.

Visit us on the Web!
StepIntoReading.com
rhcbooks.com

Educators and librarians, for a variety of teaching tools, visit us at RHTeachersLibrarians.com

ISBN 978-0-7364-4250-3 (trade) — ISBN 978-0-7364-9008-5 (lib. bdg.)
ISBN 978-0-7364-4251-0 (ebook)

Printed in the United States of America 10 9 8 7 6 5 4 3 2 1

Adapted by Sheila Sweeny Higginson

Based on an original screenplay by Evan Gore,
Heather Lombard, and Bobs Gannaway

Random House New York

A monster named Phlegm sneaks
into a baby's room at night.
The baby is the best giggler around.

If Phlegm can make her laugh,
he can gather up laugh energy.
Phlegm tries every funny trick
he knows.

But then Phlegm sneezes!

His gooey mucus gets everywhere.

It starts destroying the wall!

Back at headquarters, Phlegm tells his assistant, Maria, about the sneeze. Maria presses a giant red button, and an alarm sounds.

"Damaged Room Alert!" Celia Mae announces.

Celia Mae sends a work order to MIFT.

MIFT is the Monsters, Inc., Facilities Team.

They need to fix the damaged room.

Fritz tells Tylor and Val
to repair the room.
Tylor is nervous.
It is his first big job
as a member of MIFT.

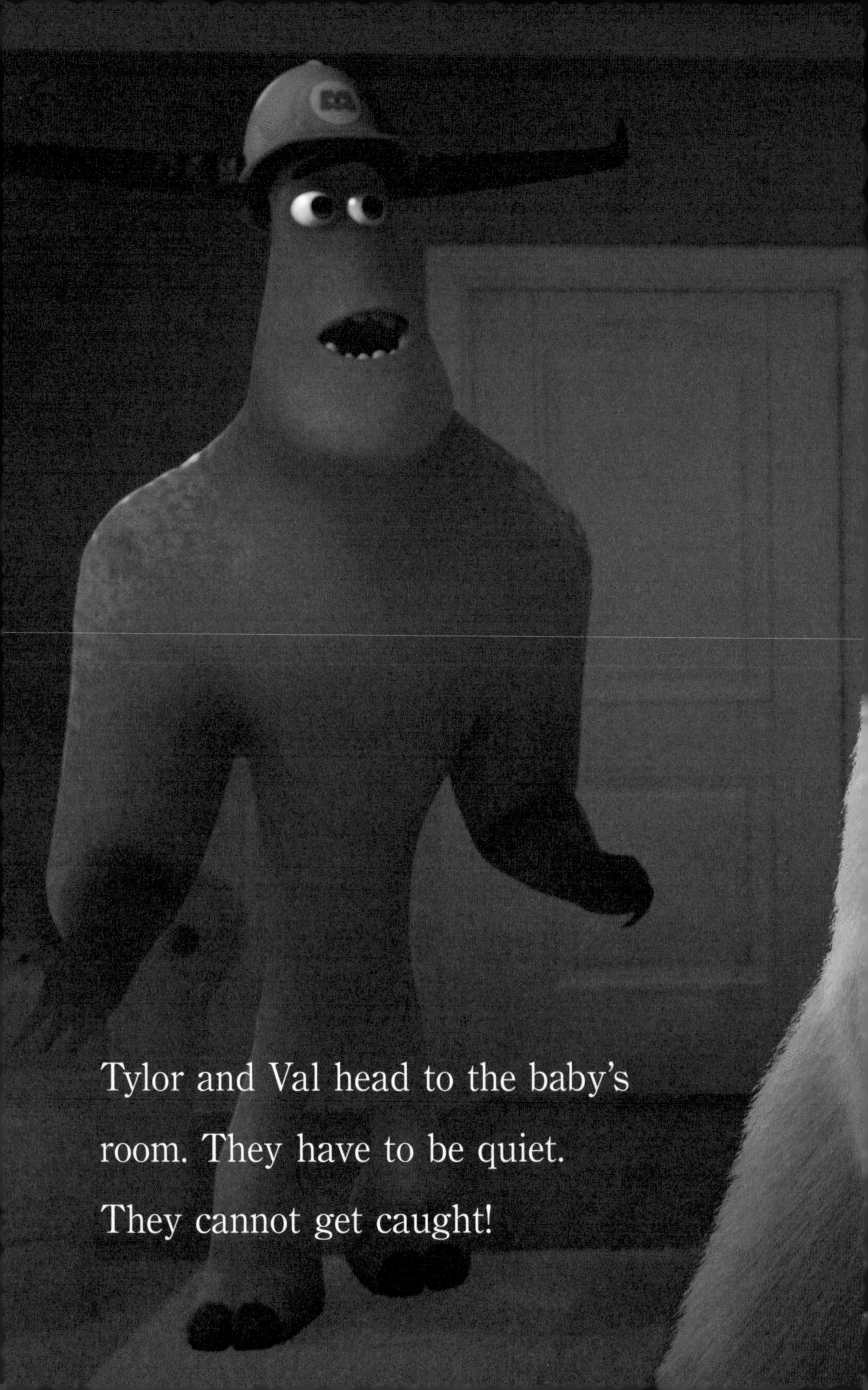

Tylor and Val head to the baby's room. They have to be quiet. They cannot get caught!

They tiptoe in and look
at the damage. It is a big job,
and they're going to need help.

Tylor gets distracted, though. He wants to get a laugh from the best giggler around!

TICKLE, TICKLE, TICKLE!

The baby wakes up.

Then the hall lights turn on.
Tylor and Val hear footsteps.
Luckily, the baby's parents
do not enter the room.

Tylor and Val sigh in relief.
But they'll have to get
the baby out of the room,
or they cannot finish the job.

The team goes to

Monsters, Inc., and tells Mike.

He does not want to bring

a kid to Monstropolis.

No kids allowed!

Celia Mae offers to babysit.

She thinks the baby is cute!

But Mike says he will watch the baby.

The group is surprised.

"I am immune to

a child's cuteness,"

Mike explains.

Mike rolls a bucket into
the baby's room.
"You're coming with me," he
whispers as he picks the baby up.

Mike carries her out of the room.

Then the MIFT team comes in.

Cutter joins Tylor and Val.

The team gets to work.

Cutter grabs a crowbar to pull off pieces
of the damaged wall.
Tylor tugs and tugs.
A piece snaps off the wall
and flies across the room.

They cannot be so noisy!

Back at Monsters, Inc., Mike has a problem. Sulley has tickets to the Monstropolis Creepees baseball game. Mike really wants to go, but what will he do with the baby?

Mike grabs his Creepees blanket
and some office supplies.
He disguises the baby as a
monster and names her Snore.
He and Sulley take her to the stadium.

Tylor, Val, and Cutter are hard at work in Snore's room.

Luckily, there's a thunderstorm outside. The team waits for thunderclaps to cover the construction noises.

Then Cutter leaves Tylor and Val
to take a lunch break!
Annoyed, Tylor kicks a soccer ball
out of the room and shuts the door.
Back on the Laugh Floor, the ball
smacks into the control panel and
deactivates the door.

The baseball game is fun
and the fans cheer loudly.
The noise upsets the baby.
Mike asks a nearby fan
to be quiet.

The fan glares at Mike.

Mike glares back.

They are about to fight, when

a ball flies toward them.

It gets closer and closer, until—

BOINK!

It hits the loud fan!

Problem solved.

In the baby's room, Val and Tylor hammer and tape and paint as quickly and quietly as they can.

ALL DONE!

Tylor heads to the closet, but one of the paint cans on his horns slips, making a loud noise!

The MIFT teammates rush to the closet. But because the door is deactivated, it is JUST A CLOSET! They can't get to Monstropolis.

Trapped in the closet, Val and Tylor worry that they'll never get back to Monsters, Inc.

Back from lunch, Cutter hits the control panel button.

The reactivated closet door opens. She saves the team!

The MIFT teammates hurry to
clean the last of their supplies
from the baby's room.
Meanwhile, Mike and Sulley
are racing back from the ball field.

Sulley praises MIFT for a job well done. Mike says goodbye to Snore and puts her in her crib.

Tylor and Val climb into the MIFT cart. That was a close call! But what started as a messy problem has ended as a fun new memory for the two MIFT pals.